For my husband James, son Alexander,
my parents Saboor and Sultana
and
Jerry the tabby cat.

Molly was making her husband James something special to eat on Valentine's Day. "I am going to make your favourite roast chicken. Have you seen Jerry?" said Molly.

Jerry was their naughty tabby cat.

Jerry limped into the kitchen looking very sorry for himself.

3

"Poor Jerry, he looks hurt," said Molly. "Perhaps we should take him to Dr Pickles the vet?"

"Don't worry, I'll take him," said James.

Molly handed over Jerry's wooden travel basket.

"Remember to fasten the door with this piece of string, otherwise Jerry might escape," Molly said.

James put the piece of string in his pocket.

Jerry didn't like going in his wooden travel basket.
He didn't like going to the vet. When they got there,
Jerry hid at the back of the basket and didn't want to come out.

Dr Pickles' waiting room smelled of dog. There were lots of strange
animal noises.

Dr Pickles greeted Jerry and James with a smile.

"So what can I do for you Jerry?" he said.

"I think Jerry has injured his paw," said James.

"This is why he's limping," Dr Pickles said, pulling out a large thorn with tweezers.

9

Jerry let out an enormous "MEEEEOOOOW."
He was not a happy tabby cat.

Dr Pickles wrapped a bandage carefully around Jerry's paw.

James bundled Jerry into the wooden travel basket. But he forgot to tie the door with the string.

Jerry pushed his way out of his basket and ran on to a very busy road.

"I can make it home myself," thought Jerry.

"Jerry, WAIT, WAIT!" shouted James. But it was too late.

Jerry had disappeared into the bushes. He stayed very still.

James decided to ring Molly and tell her what had happened.

Molly was still cooking the Valentine's Day dinner when the phone rang.

Molly knew something must be wrong, as James and Jerry had been gone for ages.

"I have some bad news. Jerry has gone missing. I forgot to fasten his basket and he escaped."

Molly was very angry with James.

"We must find him. There is going to be a big thunderstorm tonight," she said.

17

Three hours passed. James looked everywhere.

Under the cars, along the busy road and in the fields behind the vet's surgery.

He heard the distant rumble of thunder.

James thought, "Jerry is not going to like that."

Jerry was cold, wet and hungry.

"I might just stay here a bit longer, until the weather clears up," Jerry thought.

Another three hours passed. Jerry was soaked through.

His ears were wet, his whiskers were wet and his tail was wet.

He wanted to go home.

Eventually the rain stopped. Jerry decided to come out of his hiding place. In the distance he saw James.

"JERRY, JERRY," shouted James.

"Where have you been?"

Jerry let out an enormous "MEEEOW" and gave James a lick and rubbed his shins.

"Molly is going to be so happy that I found you," said James. He gave Jerry a big hug and put him safely back into the car.

When James and Jerry got home, Molly opened the front door and smiled. She gave Jerry a big hug and whispered to him softly: "We are never going to take you to the silly vet again." Jerry let out a happy "MEEOOW."

THE END

Supporter List

Saboor Mir, James Gard, Hayley Hall, Aime Baxter, Emma Faso,
Elena & Sophia Vassos Antoniou, Paula Hutchinson, Harry Fulton,
Monty Magin, Phoebe Elliott, Erin Madgwick, Rafael White O'Gara,
Maria Rather, Ben Swan, Sam Swan, Poppy Brook, Phoebe & Imogen Furmston,
Tom Potbury, Jane Myers, Zak Mir, Rachele Snowden, Rhys Belmar,
Carolyn Thompson, Charlie Watson, Anja Crombie, Clare Shildrick, Aisha Zafar,
Fawad Zafar, Mark Willis, Farhan Mir, Andrea Shead, Arif Mir, Sadaf Swan,
Abid Mir, Alana McGee, Annabel Johnson, Lachie Rennie,
Jesse Campbell, Ellie Bielby, Emily Hodgson, Victoria Haslam, Andrew Males,
Bianca Zander, Carla Jauregui, Luke & Nicola Robinson, Ben & Chloe Druett,
Barley Fields Primary School, Giselle Jauregui, Edie and Elsie Forster,
Sophia Martelli, Jessica Borrow, Lucia Raine, Alexander Gard,
Mariyum Noor Rather, Cian Morrisroe, Thorpe House School.

About The Author

Sabuhi Gard lives in Buckinghamshire with her husband James and son Alexander.

She has been a national newspaper journalist for almost 20 years,
largely writing about business news.

She was bitten by the writing bug when she was studying Classics
at King's College London in the 1990s.

After leaving university she worked as a journalist for the *Financial Times*.

Since leaving the *FT*, she has freelanced for the *Guardian*, the *Independent*,
the *Daily Express*, and ITN.

The Valentine's Day Cat is her first children's picture book for a pre-school audience.

About The Illustrator

Karen Moore lives in Eaglescliffe, Stockton-on-Tees.

She studied costume design at Wimbledon School of Art.

After leaving Wimbledon School of Art she spent time bringing up her family.

Karen now works with primary school children passing on her skills and teaching them
how to become artists in their own right.

First published in 2015 by:

Britain's Next Bestseller
An imprint of Live It Publishing
27 Old Gloucester Road
London, United Kingdom.
WC1N 3AX

www.britainsnextbestseller.co.uk

Text © Sabuhi Gard 2015
Illustrations © Karen Moore 2015

ISBN 978-1-910565-41-4 (pbk)

Printed in Poland